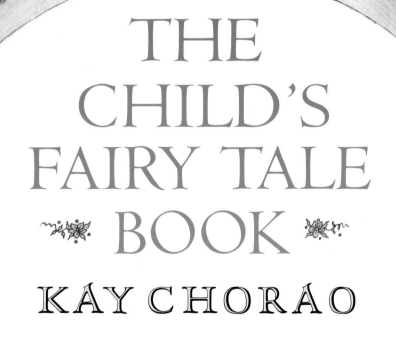

# THE
# CHILD'S
# FAIRY TALE
# BOOK

## KAY CHORAO

DUTTON CHILDREN'S BOOKS · NEW YORK

*Library of Congress Cataloging-in-Publication Data*
Chorao, Kay.
The child's fairy tale book / by Kay Chorao.—1st ed.
p.   cm.
Summary: A collection of five fairy tales including
"Snow White and the Seven Dwarfs," "Muchie Lal,"
"Rapunzel," "The Ants That Pushed on the Sky," and
"Cinderella."
ISBN 0-525-44630-3
1. Fairy tales.   [1. Fairy tales.   2. Folklore.]   I. Title.
PZ8.C457Ch   1990
398.21—dc20
[E]   89-49480   CIP   AC

Published in the United States by
Dutton Children's Books,
a division of Penguin Books USA Inc.
Designer: Riki Levinson

Printed in Hong Kong by South China Printing Co.
First Edition   10 9 8 7 6 5 4 3 2 1

This book belongs to

_____

# Contents

# Snow White
## and the Seven Dwarfs

Once on a snowy winter day a queen sat sewing at her window. As she looked out at the snowflakes falling like white feathers from the sky, she pricked her finger. Three drops of blood fell on the white snow.

"How beautiful the red is against the white snow, on the black of the ebony windowsill," said the Queen. "If only I had a child with skin as white as snow, lips as red as blood, and hair as black as ebony."

And as it happened, such a daughter was born to the Queen, and she was named Snow White. But soon after the royal birth, the Queen died.

When a year had passed, the King married again. This queen was very beautiful but proud and haughty.

Every day the new queen stood before her mirror and said, "Mirror, mirror on the wall, who is fairest of us all?"

Then the mirror, which was magical, would answer her, "Queen, thou art fairest of us all!"

The Queen was then content because the mirror spoke only the truth.

As Snow White grew, she became more and more lovely. One day when the Queen asked the mirror who was most fair, the mirror replied, "Queen, thou art the fairest in this hall, but Snow White is fairer than us all."

These words filled the Queen with rage and envy. Each day she watched the child's beauty grow, and each day her anger and jealousy increased.

Finally the Queen called one of her huntsmen and commanded him, "Take the child far into the forest and kill her, and bring me her lung and liver as a token."

The huntsman obediently took Snow White into the forest, but despite the Queen's order, he could not kill her. The girl begged to be allowed to escape into the woods and never return.

"Run away, then, my poor child," the huntsman said, thinking sadly that she would surely be eaten by wild beasts. He left her there and returned to the Queen with the lung and liver of a wild boar.

Snow White ran deep into the great forest, past towering trees with gnarled branches, over sharp rocks and past wild beasts in the black shadows. She ran on and on until she came to a clearing. And in this clearing was a little cottage.

Snow White knocked on the door, but there was no reply. She tried the door, and it opened, so she went inside. A table was set with seven little plates and seven little knives, forks, and spoons on a white linen cloth. Seven little beds stood against the wall.

Snow White ate some bread and vegetables from each of the plates and took a sip from each of the mugs. She tried each of the beds and finally lay down on the seventh one and fell asleep.

When it grew dark, the owners of the cottage returned. They were seven dwarfs, who worked all day in the mountains, digging for gold and precious stones.

As they entered their home, each holding a lantern, they saw that someone had been in their cottage.

The first said, "Who has been sitting on my chair?"

The second said, "Who has been eating from my plate?"

The third said, "Who has been eating my bread?"

The fourth said, "Who has been eating my vegetables?"

The fifth said, "Who has been using my knife?"

The sixth said, "Who has been using my fork?"

The seventh said, "Who has been drinking from my mug?"

10

Then the first dwarf noticed that his bed was rumpled. And one after another the other dwarfs asked, "Who has been sleeping in my bed?"

But when the seventh dwarf reached his bed, he found Snow White fast asleep.

"Look who's in my bed!" he called out.

The others ran to his bedside and held their lanterns high over the sleeping child.

"How beautiful she is," they whispered. "Let her sleep."

When morning came, Snow White awoke and felt frightened of the little dwarfs. But they spoke kindly to her and asked how she had found their cottage. When Snow White told them what had happened, the dwarfs were filled with pity for the girl and suggested that she live with them.

And so each day Snow White cleaned the cottage and cooked while the dwarfs marched off to the mines. But before leaving each day they warned her, "Whatever you do, you must not let anyone in because your wicked stepmother may discover where you are."

Snow White promised, and she became very happy in her new life.

Meanwhile the Queen thought Snow White was dead and was certain that she was now the fairest of all. But one day she stood before the mirror and said, "Mirror, mirror on the wall, who is fairest of us all?"

And the mirror answered, "Queen, thou art the fairest that I see, but over the hills, where the seven dwarfs dwell, Snow White is still alive and well, and there is none so fair as she."

The Queen was greatly angered. So she disguised herself as an old peddler woman who called at people's houses selling things from a basket. Dressed so that no one could recognize her, she set off to find Snow White.

"Lovely things for sale," she called when she reached the dwarfs' cottage.

Snow White looked out a window.

"Good day, dear lady. What do you sell?" she asked.

"Bodice laces of all colors," said the peddler.

Snow White thought there could be no harm in allowing the old woman in. So she unbolted the door and let her bring the basket of laces inside.

"Come, let me lace you up properly," said the old woman.

Snow White was not suspicious and allowed her to draw the laces. The wicked woman pulled them so tight that they took Snow White's breath away. She fell to the floor as if she were dead.

In the evening, the dwarfs found Snow White lying on the floor. They lifted her up tenderly and cut the laces. Soon she began to breathe, and color returned to her cheeks.

The dwarfs knew at once that the peddler woman was Snow White's stepmother, so they warned her again to take care and never allow anyone into the cottage.

But when the wicked queen got back to the castle, she stood before her mirror and asked, "Mirror, mirror on the wall, who is fairest of us all?"

It answered, "Queen, thou art the fairest that I see, but over the hills, where the seven dwarfs dwell, Snow White is still alive and well, and there is none so fair as she."

So once more, in a rage, the Queen began to plot Snow White's death. This time she dressed as a beggar woman bearing a basket of combs with poisoned teeth.

"Lovely things for sale!" sang the beggar woman once she reached the dwarfs' cottage door.

"I am not allowed to let you in," said Snow White.

"But surely you may look," said the old woman. She took out a comb and held it up.

Snow White opened the door and allowed the old woman to put the comb in her hair. And no sooner had the comb been placed in her black locks than Snow White fell to the floor of the cottage, as if dead.

Fortunately, it was evening, so the dwarfs soon returned. When they saw Snow White on the floor, they knew that she had been tricked again by her stepmother. Quickly they discovered the comb and plucked it from her head, and Snow White recovered.

At home the Queen again went to her mirror, and again it told her that Snow White was alive and still the fairest in the land.

This time the wicked queen shook with fury. Then she went to a secret chamber and concocted a poisoned apple. On the outside it looked delicious, but inside it was deadly.

The Queen disguised herself as a farmer's wife, returned to the dwarfs' cottage, and knocked on the door.

"I cannot let anyone in," said Snow White.

"Then I will go away," said the farmer's wife, "but I will leave you one of my apples."

"I am afraid to take it," said Snow White.

"Look," wheedled the farmer's wife, cutting the apple in two. "I will eat the green half. You may have the rosy red part." She took a bite from the green part, knowing that all the poison was in the red side of the apple.

Assured that the apple was harmless, Snow White took a bite and immediately fell down senseless.

This time when the Queen returned home and stood before her mirror, it told her, "Queen, thou art the fairest of us all." And the Queen was satisfied.

Back at the cottage, the dwarfs found Snow White lying on the floor. They tried everything they could think of to wake her, but to no avail.

The dwarfs were heartbroken. They wept and mourned for three days and three nights. Then they made Snow White a coffin of glass and set it on the mountainside, keeping vigil over it at all times.

One day a king's son rode past the glass coffin and saw Snow White inside, her skin still as white as snow, her lips as red as blood, and her hair as black as ebony. He read the gold inscription on the coffin, which told Snow White's name and said that she was a king's daughter.

The Prince was touched by Snow White's beauty, and he begged to take the coffin to his castle, where he would cherish and guard Snow White with his life.

The dwarfs took pity on the Prince and reluctantly granted his request.

As the Prince's servants were carrying the coffin down the mountainside, they stumbled on the rocky surface. The coffin was jarred, and the piece of apple fell from Snow White's mouth. In a little while she opened her eyes and lifted the lid of the coffin.

"Where am I?" she cried.

The Prince, overjoyed, told Snow White what had happened. Then he begged her to come with him and be his wife, and Snow White gladly accepted.

So a magnificent wedding was planned. One of the guests was the wicked queen, who once more consulted her mirror as she was dressing for the wedding feast.

"Who is fairest of us all?" she asked.

The mirror answered, "Queen, thou art the fairest in this hall, but the young princess is fairer than us all."

These words angered the Queen so deeply that she almost did not go to the wedding. But she was so curious to see the young princess that she could not stay away.

When she stepped into the great hall and recognized Snow White, her rage was so great and so violent that she had to be taken away. She died soon after.

But Snow White and the Prince were wed and lived happily forever after.

# Muchie Lal

East Indian

A long time ago, in East India, there lived a rajah and ranee who had no children. They prayed to the gods for a son, but their prayers were not answered.

One day a number of fish were delivered for the Rajah's dinner. One was still living, so a palace maid slipped it into a basin of water. The Ranee passed by the dining hall and noticed the little fish.

"How pretty!" she said. "I shall keep it as a pet."

And so the fish was named the Muchie Rajah, which means the Fish Prince, and the Ranee lavished tender affection on him. She fed him boiled rice twice a day, and as he grew, she provided him with larger and larger tanks so that he might splash and swim in comfort. He grew so huge that stories spread about the fish's tremendous size and terrible strength.

One morning when the Ranee brought him his rice, the Muchie Rajah called out, "Queen Mother, I am so lonely swimming by myself. Cannot you find me a wife?"

The Ranee was surprised to hear her fish speak, but she promised to find him a wife.

She sent messengers among her people asking for a young girl to come and be the bride of her Muchie Rajah. But the people all answered, "We cannot give one of our daughters to be devoured by a great fish."

The Ranee was so devoted to her pet that she offered a bag of gold to anyone who would bring the Muchie Rajah a wife. But in village after village, the people refused. Even the beggars refused to offer their daughters, fearing that they would end as a meal for the fish.

Then one day the wife of a fakir heard about the offer. This wife hated her little stepdaughter, whom she saw as a rival to her own child.

"Give me the bag of gold, and take my daughter," she said to the Ranee's messenger. She snatched the gold and sent the girl to bathe and prepare herself for the Ranee's court.

The stepdaughter saw no escape, since her father was traveling far from home. She went sorrowfully to the river and wept bitterly as she washed her saree. Her tears fell into the hole where a seven-headed cobra lived.

The cobra poked his heads out of the riverbank and watched the girl. "Little girl, why do you cry?" he asked kindly.

"Oh, sir, my stepmother has sold me to the Ranee. I am to be the wife of the Muchie Rajah, and I know he will eat me up."

The cobra was a wise creature. He thought a moment and said, "Do not be afraid, my daughter. The Muchie Rajah has been enchanted by angry gods. He was not always a fish. Once he was a handsome prince. Take these three small stones and tie them in the corner of your saree. When you enter your new home, do not fall asleep or the Muchie Rajah will eat you up. If you see him rushing at you, throw this stone at him and he will sink to the bottom of the tank. Do the same with the second and third stones, and you will be safe."

The fakir's daughter took the stones and thanked the cobra, who disappeared down his hole. She had little faith that pebbles would be useful, but she hid them in her saree as the cobra advised.

When the girl arrived at court, the Ranee welcomed her warmly and helped her into a basket, which was lowered to a room at the edge of a large fish tank. The Ranee had decorated the girl's room with thick carpets and curtains of delicate silk. At least I am away from my stepmother's cruelty and the endless chores, the girl thought. Perhaps I will be happy here.

Her hopes vanished when suddenly a rush of waves and water dashed against the threshold of her door, and she saw the Muchie Rajah coming toward her with his great jaws wide open.

Quickly the fakir's daughter seized the first pebble from her saree and threw it at the great fish. He sank to the bottom of the tank. But he rose and rushed toward her, so she threw the second pebble, and again he sank. He came at her a third time, even more fiercely. With all her might, she threw the third pebble.

No sooner did it touch him than the spell was broken and there stood a handsome young prince.

The girl was so startled that she began to cry. The Prince thanked her gently for breaking the spell cast over him, and he asked if she would consent to be the Muchie Ranee.

When news of the transformation spread, there was great rejoicing, and the new prince and princess were married. Then they settled happily in the royal palace.

The Muchie Ranee's stepmother came often to see her stepdaughter and pretended to be delighted at the girl's good fortune. The young ranee forgave her stepmother's past cruelty and always received her kindly.

Then one day, encouraged by her stepmother, the Ranee decided to visit her father, whom she missed very much.

"Do not stay long, because there will be no happiness for me until you return," said the Prince.

"No, I will not stay long," said the Ranee, and off she went to her father's little village.

Once the Ranee was there, the stepmother instructed her own daughter to invite the Ranee to the riverbank.

"Beg her to allow you to try on her jewels, then give her a push and drown her in the river," commanded the step-mother.

The girl followed her mother's instructions and pushed her stepsister into the river. Then she ran to her mother. "Here are the jewels, Mother, and my stepsister will trouble us no longer."

But it happened that just when the Muchie Ranee fell into the river, the seven-headed cobra was swimming nearby. He saw the little princess plunge deep into the river, and he rescued her and carried her safely to his home on the river-bank.

Meanwhile, the fakir's wicked wife dressed her daughter in the Ranee's jewels and took her to the palace. "I have brought back your wife, safe and sound," she said to the Prince.

The Rajah looked at the girl and thought, This does not look like my wife. But the room was dark and she was well disguised, so he said nothing.

When daylight came, though, he saw that he had been deceived. "My wife was bright and cheerful. She had pretty, loving ways and merry words. This is not she!" He took the jewels from the sullen girl and sent her away. Then he commanded that the stepmother be found. "Unless she can tell me where my wife is," he said, "I will have her hanged." But the fakir's wife had disappeared.

Unaware of all this, the little Muchie Ranee continued to live with the cobra family. They treated her with kindness. There was nothing the cobra would not do for the Ranee. But she was not allowed to try to find her way back to her husband.

"No, I will not let you go," said the cobra. "It is too dangerous. If your husband comes here and finds you, it is well, but you cannot wander around alone in search of him."

When the Ranee bore a son, he grew up alongside the young cobras as if they were all brothers and sisters. The Ranee named her son Muchie Lal, which means Ruby Fish, and he was a lovely child, brave and cheerful.

When Muchie Lal was about three years old, a bangle seller came by, and the Muchie Ranee bought bangles for the child's wrists and ankles. He was a lively child and broke the bangles in play. So the next day his mother bought him more, and even more the following day.

Meanwhile, the Muchie Rajah was looking for the Ranee everywhere. He searched every part of the country for his dear wife. On his travels he met a bangle seller, who happened to mention that he had sold many bangles to a family living in a cobra's hole.

The odd tale caught the Rajah's attention. "Who were these people?" he asked.

"A woman, and a child about three years old. He is the most beautiful child I have ever seen," said the seller. "His name is Muchie Lal."

The Muchie Rajah then grabbed the bangle seller by the shoulders and asked excitedly, "My good man, where were these people? Pray take me to them!"

So the following day, the old seller took the Rajah to the place where he had seen the little boy and the cobras.

The bangle seller jangled his wares, and a gentle voice came from inside the cobra's hole. "Come here, my Muchie Lal, and try on your bangles."

The Muchie Rajah dropped to his knees beside the hole and said, "Oh, wife, show your beautiful face to me."

At the sound of his voice the Princess ran out. "Husband, husband! You have found me!"

It was a joyful reunion, and even the cobras, who would miss the Ranee and her child, were filled with happiness when they saw the radiant young couple reunited.

And they were never parted again.

# Rapunzel

nce upon a time there lived a man and wife who had long wished for a child. These good people had a little window at the back of their house that overlooked a magnificent garden filled with flowers and herbs. But the garden was surrounded by a high wall, and no one dared to enter it because it belonged to a powerful witch, who was feared by all.

One day the wife stood at the window and looked down on the garden. In one of the vegetable beds she saw the most beautiful lettuce, of the kind called rapunzel. It looked so tempting that she longed to eat some.

Every day that followed, she looked out her window at the fresh, green lettuce, and the more she looked at it, the more she longed to eat it. Soon she began to look pale and miserable because her craving was so great.

"Dear wife, are you ill?" asked her husband.

"Oh, husband," she answered, "if I do not get some of that fresh lettuce, I know I shall die."

The husband, who loved his wife dearly, said to himself, Whatever the cost, I must climb into the witch's garden and fetch some rapunzel.

So at twilight the man clambered over the wall and picked a handful of lettuce, which he brought to his wife. She made a salad, which was so delicious that she craved even more. And so, the next night at dusk, the husband scaled the wall again.

This time the witch was waiting for him. "How dare you climb into my garden, stealing lettuce like a thief?" she said angrily. "You shall pay for this."

"Please have mercy," cried the man. "My wife longed so much for the lettuce that without it she would have pined away and died."

The witch's anger was softened a little. "If it's as you say, you may take as much as you like," she said. "But there is one condition. You must give me the child your wife will soon bring into the world."

The poor man was so frightened that he agreed. And no sooner had his wife given birth to a child than the witch appeared and took possession of the tiny girl, whom she named Rapunzel.

As she grew, Rapunzel became the most beautiful child under the sun, with wonderful long hair, as fine as spun gold. When she was twelve years old, the witch locked her in a tower in the middle of a great forest. This tower had neither doors nor stairs, but at the top there was one small window. If the witch wanted to get inside, she came and stood underneath and called,

> Rapunzel, Rapunzel,
> Let down your hair.

When Rapunzel heard the witch, she unfastened her braids, wound them around a hook, and let the long plaits fall out the window to the ground below. Then the old witch climbed up the braids to the tower window.

Then one day a prince rode through the forest near the tower, and he heard the sound of singing. It was Rapunzel, singing to fill her solitude. The sound was so sweet that the Prince listened spellbound.

He wanted to see who sang so wonderfully and followed her voice to the tower. But he could find no door, so he rode away.

Yet the Prince was haunted by the lovely song and returned every day to listen. One day when he was standing behind a tree, listening, he saw the witch come along and heard her call,

Rapunzel, Rapunzel,
Let down your hair.

Rapunzel let down her braids and the witch climbed up.

"So that's the staircase," said the Prince. "Then I, too, will climb it and try my luck."

On the following day, at dusk, the Prince went to the tower and cried,

Rapunzel, Rapunzel,
Let down your hair.

Immediately the golden hair came tumbling down, and the Prince climbed up.

At first Rapunzel was terribly frightened when the Prince appeared. Aside from the witch, he was the first person she had ever seen. But the Prince spoke kindly and told how her singing had touched his heart, and soon Rapunzel lost her fear. And when he asked if she would take him for her husband, she thought, He is kind and handsome and will love me better than my old godmother. And so she said yes.

Then she thought a moment and said, "I will need a way to escape from this tower, so you must bring a skein of silk with you each time you come to see me. I will braid it into a ladder."

And so every evening the Prince came to Rapunzel, each time bringing silk.

The witch knew nothing of this until one day Rapunzel said without thinking, "How is it, godmother, that you feel so much heavier than the Prince?"

"Oh, you wicked child!" cried the witch. "I thought I had hidden you from the whole world, yet you have managed to deceive me."

In her fury, the witch seized a pair of scissors and, snip snap, cut off Rapunzel's beautiful hair. Then she took the girl to a lonely desert, where she left her to live in misery.

That night the witch returned to the tower. She fastened Rapunzel's braids to the hook in the window frame, and when the Prince came and called,

> Rapunzel, Rapunzel,
> Let down your hair,

she let the braids down.

The Prince climbed up and found not his beloved Rapunzel but the old witch, who looked at him with eyes that glittered with rage. "You came for your lady love, but the pretty bird has flown and its song has been silenced. The cat caught it and will scratch your eyes out, too. You will never see Rapunzel again."

The Prince was filled with grief, and in his despair, he jumped from the tower. He landed safely in a bush, but his eyes were pierced by its thorns so that he was blinded. He wandered pitifully about the forest, living on roots and berries and lamenting the loss of his bride.

For a year the Prince wandered, until one day he came to the desert. Suddenly he heard a voice that seemed familiar. He walked toward the sound of the singing, and as he came closer, Rapunzel saw and recognized him. As she put her arms around his neck and wept, two of her tears moistened his eyes and they were magically healed, so he could see as well as before.

Then the Prince led Rapunzel to his kingdom, where they were welcomed with joy and lived happily for the rest of their years.

# The Ants
## That Pushed on the Sky

Native American

In the land of the Pueblos there once lived a
brave young Indian named Kahp-too-oo-yoo, or Cornstalk-
Young-Man. He was a famous hunter and a great wizard with
power over the clouds. When Kahp-too-oo-yoo willed it, the
rains fell and made the dry fields dance with tender green
shoots.

Kahp-too-oo-yoo had a friend who often explored and
hunted with him. But the friend was false at heart. This
young man was also a wizard, but he kept his powers secret.

One day the two young men went hunting. They rose at
sunrise and walked deep into the wood, where they spotted a
herd of deer. Kahp-too-oo-yoo followed part of the herd
northwest, and his friend went southeast. At day's end Kahp-
too-oo-yoo returned to the spot where they had parted, carrying a deer. But his friend returned empty-handed.

"Come, friend," said Kahp-too-oo-yoo, "let us share like brothers. Take part of this deer and carry it to your house, as if you had killed it."

"No, thank you," said the other. He remained silent as the two gathered firewood and then returned home.

Kahp-too-oo-yoo was greeted joyfully by his sisters, who praised his hunting skill and prepared the deer for cooking.

The friend was still sullen the next time the two went hunting, and even more so the third time, because each day only Kahp-too-oo-yoo returned with a deer.

On the fourth hunting trip, Kahp-too-oo-yoo again returned with a deer on his shoulders and found his friend waiting for him empty-handed.

"Kahp-too-oo-yoo, I wish you to prove that you are truly my friend, for I think you are not," said the sullen young man.

"I will gladly do anything to prove my friendship," said Kahp-too-oo-yoo.

"Will you play a game by which I will test you?" said the friend.

"Of course I will," said Kahp-too-oo-yoo.

"Then climb this broken pine tree that has one great arm twisting to the sky, and pretend that the tree limb is a horse," said the friend.

So, in good faith, Kahp-too-oo-yoo climbed the tree and
rode on the swinging limb. But the false friend cast a spell
upon the branch, and it grew so fast that it shot up high into
the sky, carrying Kahp-too-oo-yoo out of sight.

The false friend took Kahp-too-oo-yoo's deer and returned
to the village.

"Where is our brother?" asked Kahp-too-oo-yoo's sisters.

"He did not come to our meeting place. Surely he will
return soon," said the sly young man.

The sisters and their old parents waited and waited, but Kahp-too-oo-yoo did not return. His family wept, and all the village mourned. With Kahp-too-oo-yoo gone, there was no rain, and soon the crops grew yellow in the fields and the animals grew weak and listless. In time the crops turned brown and withered, the animals collapsed from thirst, and the people of the village began to weaken and die.

At last the poor old father assembled his family and said, "We must try to find Kahp-too-oo-yoo. I will travel south. Mother will travel east. Older sister will travel north, and younger sister will travel west." And this they did.

As Blue-Corn-Maiden, who was the older sister, traveled further and further north, she heard a faint song coming softly, sadly through the high tree branches. She held her breath and listened:

> Old-Black-Cane
> My father is called;
> Corn Woman
> My mother is called.

Blue-Corn-Maiden recognized the names of her own parents and the voice of her brother, Kahp-too-oo-yoo. She brought her sister and parents to hear, too, and they followed the plaintive song until they reached the base of the old pine tree. There they found the young hunter's bow and arrows lying on the ground and his pack of firewood fastened with rawhide, as he always tied it to carry home.

"He must be near," they said. They searched the forest all around the pine tree but could see no further sign of Kahp-too-oo-yoo. So, with heavy hearts, they finally went home.

One day Little Black Ant, who lived at the base of the tree, took a journey up the bewitched pine, to its very top. When he found Kahp-too-oo-yoo, he was astonished.

"Why are you here, while your people are suffering and dying in the drought below?" he asked.

"I am not here of my free will. I am here because of the jealousy of he who was as my brother," said Kahp-too-oo-yoo. "The tree was bewitched and I along with it. And now I am dying here of famine."

"If that is so," said Little Black Ant, "I will help you."

Then he ran down the pine tree and into the world to summon all those of his nation and of the nation of the Big Red Ants. Soon all the armies of the Little Black Ants and the Big Red Ants met at the foot of the pine and held a council.

It was agreed that the Big Red Ants would climb the lower part of the tree, the Little Black Ants would climb the higher part, and together they would form a ladder up the pine tree all the way to the sky. This they did, and they passed along a cup made from the top of an acorn, which held cornmeal, water, and honey.

Kahp-too-oo-yoo drank from the tiny cup, which magically refilled itself, until he satisfied his hunger and thirst.

"Now, friend," said the leader of the Little Black Ants, "you must shut your eyes until I say 'Ahw!' "

The young hunter shut his eyes, and the Little Black Ants above him put their feet against the sky and pushed with all their might, and the Big Red Ants below him caught the trunk of the pine tree and pulled as hard as they could, and the great pine bent a quarter of its length toward the earth.

"Ahw!" shouted Little Black Ant.

Kahp-too-oo-yoo opened his eyes but could see nothing below.

"We will try again," said the ant, sending the signal to his troops.

Again they tried, and this time Kahp-too-oo-yoo could begin to see the scorched brown land, far below.

For a third time, the ants pushed and pulled with all their might, and this great effort brought the young man so close to earth that he could see his own village, filled with dying people.

A fourth effort by the ants put Kahp-too-oo-yoo onto the earth, soft with pine needles. He thanked the ants for their great kindness, and killed a deer so they might eat and replenish their strength.

Before going to his village, Kahp-too-oo-yoo fashioned a flute from the bark of a tree and played a joyful song. Clouds formed in the skies and the rain fell onto the brown earth, instantly turning it green and plentiful.

The villagers could scarcely believe their ears when they heard the rain pounding on the earth and making music on their roofs. They came out and turned their faces to the heavens. The dead and dying returned to health, as did the animals lying in the fields. And the whole village ran through the healing rains to welcome Kahp-too-oo-yoo. The people wept for joy, and when they returned to their homes they found their storerooms brimming with grain and corn.

So everyone gathered for a feast of roasted corn and ate and danced and sang. As for the false friend, he died of shame in his house, and no one wept for him.

# Cinderella

here once lived a rich man whose wife lay ill. Knowing she was close to death, she called her daughter to her bedside. "Dear child," she said, "be kind and good, and I will look down upon you from heaven."

The woman died soon after, and her daughter went every day to the snow-covered grave and wept, too grieved to notice the cold. But when spring came, melting the snow away, the man took a new wife.

The stepmother was a haughty, cruel woman, with two daughters who resembled her in every way. They too were haughty in appearance, and bitter and ugly at heart. They took away their little stepsister's pretty dresses, made her wear rags and wooden shoes, and put her to work as their kitchen-maid.

"Look at the proud princess now," they laughed while the girl worked from morning until night, drawing water, making fires, cooking and scrubbing. To torment her further, the stepsisters threw peas and lentils among the ashes and made her pick them up. When night came, she was forced to sleep on the hearth among the cinders. Because she always looked dusty and dirty, they called her Cinderella.

One day the father went to a fair, but before he left, he asked what his stepdaughters wanted him to bring back.

"Fine clothes," said one.

"Pearls and jewels," said the other.

"And what will you have?" he asked Cinderella.

"The first twig that strikes against your hat on the way home, Father."

So he brought the stepdaughters fine clothing and jewels, and for Cinderella he brought the twig of a hazel tree. She thanked her father and took the twig to her mother's grave, where she planted it. Kneeling by the grave, she wept bitterly, and the twig, watered by her tears, began to grow.

Cinderella went often to her mother's grave, where her tears watered the twig until it grew into a fine tree. And each time she wept upon the tree, a white dove rose out of the branches.

One day it was announced that the King was to hold a three-day festival. All the young women of the country were invited, so that the King's son might choose a bride.

The stepsisters could think of nothing but the ball, where they would see the Prince. "Comb our hair. Brush our shoes," they ordered Cinderella. "We are going to the royal ball."

"Could I go, too?" asked Cinderella.

"You, Cinderella?" said the stepmother. "In all your dust and dirt, you want to go to the festival?"

The girl persisted, so the stepmother said at last, "I will throw a dish of lentils in the ashes. If you can pick them all up in two hours, you may go with us."

Cinderella went off to her mother's grave and called out,

> O gentle doves, O turtledoves,
> And all the birds that be,
> The lentils that in ashes lie
> Come and pick up for me!
> > The good must be put in the dish,
> > The bad you may eat if you wish.

And from the skies a flock of white birds fluttered down and began to pick, peck, pick among the ashes. They put all the good lentils in the dish within an hour and flew away.

Cinderella ran to her stepmother and joyfully held out the dish.

"No, Cinderella, you may not go to the ball. You have no proper clothes and you do not know how to dance. Everyone would laugh at you!"

But the girl cried in disappointment, so the stepmother added, "If you can pick two dishes of lentils from the ashes, you may come," thinking this was an impossible task.

For a second time Cinderella called the birds from the sky. Two white doves and a flock of turtledoves descended and pick, peck, picked all the lentils from the ashes.

But still the stepmother told Cinderella that she could not go, and swept out the door with her two proud daughters.

Cinderella ran to her mother's grave and cried,

Little tree, little tree, shake over me
That silver and gold may come down and cover me.

From the hazel tree a dove flew down with a dress of gold and silver and a pair of silver slippers embroidered with silk. Cinderella dressed in the finery and ran to the festival ball.

The Prince noticed her at once and led her onto the dance floor, where he refused to share her with any other partner. She was recognized by no one, but admired for her grace and beauty by all.

When the evening ended, Cinderella slipped away. The Prince followed her, but she hid in her father's pigeon house.

The next night the festival began anew, and again Cinderella went to the hazel tree by her mother's grave.

Little tree, little tree, shake over me,
That silver and gold may come down and cover me.

The dove flew down with a dress more splendid than before, and when Cinderella appeared at the festival, she was even more radiant and beautiful.

The Prince was waiting for her and for a second time would share her with no other partner.

When the evening ended, Cinderella tried to leave unseen, but again the Prince followed her. This time she ran to the garden behind her house, climbed into a pear tree, and hid among the branches.

On the third day, Cinderella returned to her mother's grave and spoke to the hazel tree.

Little tree, little tree, shake over me,
That silver and gold may come down and cover me.

This time the dress was even more exquisite, and the slippers were pure gold. When she appeared at the festival, people were astonished by her beauty and stared in wonder.

The Prince danced with her alone, and if anyone else asked
to dance with her, he replied, "She is *my* partner."

When evening fell, the Prince was prepared to stop this mysterious maiden's flight. He had a sticky tar spread on the steps, so that when she ran off, one of her golden shoes stuck and was left behind. He picked it up, and the next morning he set out to find its owner, stating that she would be his bride.

When the Prince reached Cinderella's house, the elder stepsister rushed to try on the shoe. She could not get her great toe in, as the shoe was too small, so her mother handed her a knife and said, "Cut off the toe. When you are Queen, you will never go on foot."

So the girl cut off her toe and squeezed her foot into the shoe. The Prince took her with him on the horse, and they rode away.

But as they passed by the grave, two doves in the hazel tree cried,

> There they go, there they go!
> There is blood on her shoe,
> The shoe is too small,
> —Not the right bride at all!

The Prince looked at the shoe and saw the blood flowing. So he turned the horse around and took the false bride back.

The younger stepsister then tried on the shoe, but her heel was too large.

"Cut off a piece of your heel," said the stepmother. She handed the girl a knife, so the stepsister cut off her heel and pushed her foot into the shoe. The Prince placed her on his horse, and again they rode by the hazel tree. The doves cried out from the branches,

> There they go, there they go!
> There is blood on her shoe,
> The shoe is too small,
> —Not the right bride at all!

Then the Prince looked down and saw that the birds spoke the truth, so he returned the girl to her home.

"This is not the right one," he said. "Have you no other daughter?"

"No," said the stepmother, "only an ignorant little kitchenmaid. She could not possibly be your bride."

But the Prince ordered that this girl be brought before him.

"Oh, no, she is much too dirty," said the stepmother. "I could not let her be seen."

But the Prince insisted, and Cinderella was called. She washed her face and hands and went to the Prince, who held out the golden shoe.

Cinderella took off her wooden shoe and slipped her foot easily into the gold one. It fit perfectly. And when the Prince looked carefully at her face, he knew that he had found his beautiful, mysterious maiden.

"This is the right bride!" he exclaimed.

The stepmother and sisters grew pale with anger and envy as the Prince lifted Cinderella onto his horse and they rode off in great joy.

As they passed the hazel tree, the white doves sang,

> There they go, there they go!
> No blood on her shoe,
> The shoe's not too small,
> She's the right bride after all!